Samantha Smartypants
Runs for
Class President

To Rebecca,
Vote for Samantha!!
Barbara Puccia

D0167711

Samantha Smartypants
Runs for
Class President

by Barbara Puccia

Cover Illustrated by Emma Kane
Content Illustrated by Natalie Puccia

This is a work of fiction. Names, characters, places, and incidents either are the product of the author's imagination or are used fictitiously. Any resemblance to actual persons, living or dead, events, or locales is entirely coincidental.

Copyright © 2014 by Barbara Puccia
Cover illustrations copyright © 2014 by Barbara Puccia
Content illustrations copyright © 2014 by Barbara Puccia

All rights reserved. Self-published in the United States through CreateSpace, an Amazon company. No part of this publication may be reproduced in whole or in part, or stored in a retrieval system, or transmitted in any form or by any means, electronic, mechanical, photocopying, recording, or otherwise, without written permission of the author. For information regarding permissions, write to Barbara Puccia, 36 Mohawk Drive, Ramsey, NJ 07446 or email at samanthasmartypants@gmail.com.

ISBN-13:978-1495280832
ISBN-10:1495280837

Summary: To her surprise, Samantha gets nominated for third grade class president. Although she's really smart, she has to do all kinds of things that make her really nervous. She'll need to give a speech, make a poster, and worst of all run against the most popular kids in class. Will she make it?

Contents

CHAPTER 1

CLASS PRESIDENT

Ms. Thompson looked so excited, you'd think she just won a million bucks.

"Boys and girls," she said, "we're going to have an election. Just like when your parents vote for the president of the United States. You're going to elect a class president."

"Awesome!" Lisa Logan said, turning to her best friend, Deena Jackson.

"Cool," said Bobby Stanger to his friend, Tommy Tagaloney.

I didn't know if an election was such a good idea, so I didn't say anything.

1

Ms. Thompson continued. "The president will have special jobs, like bringing the attendance sheets to the office, and suggesting new ideas for our class."

"Like no more homework!" Bobby said to Tommy. They gave each other a high five.

"Like tank-top Tuesdays," Lisa said to Deena.

I couldn't think of any ideas because things ran pretty well in our third grade class already.

Ms. Thompson picked up an old shoebox from her desk. It was painted red and white, with the word "NOMINATIONS" in big blue letters on the side, and a large slit on top.

"If you think someone will make a good president, write that person's name down on a piece of paper and place it in this box. That's a nomination. Each student nominated will have one week to campaign."

"I went to CAMP and it wasn't in PAIN," said Deena.

I raised my hand.

"Campaign means you tell the class why they should vote for you," I said.

"That's right," said Ms. Thompson.

"Samantha Smartypants!" said Bobby.

That's not my real name. It's really Samantha Pojanowski. Some kids call me Samantha Smartypants instead. That's because in September, Bobby got mad when I got 100 on all my tests and answered all Ms. Thompson's questions. He called me Smartypants and the name stuck. At first, it bothered me, but now I just ignore it.

"Shhh," said Ms. Thompson. "When you're nominated you can make posters to hang up and flyers to hand out. You'll also give a speech."

"In front of the whole class!" shouted Lisa. Her eyes lit up, like a great big lightning bug.

A speech, I thought. That's scary. I wouldn't want to do that.

"Uh, how long is the speech?" Bobby asked.

"One or two minutes," said Ms. Thompson.

Bobby looked at Tommy who gave him a thumbs-up and said, "No big deal."

"Next Friday will be Election Day," she said. "Each student will vote by checking off one of the names on a ballot.

She wrote the word on the board. "BALLOT."

"Hey I go to BALLET," yelled Lisa. "I'm in a dance recital next month."

"Not ballet, Lisa. Ballot, with an 'O', not an 'E'."

Ms. Thompson drew a rectangle. She wrote three names in it. "Mickey", "Minnie" and "Donald." Next to each, she added a little square box.

"If you want to vote for Minnie, you check the box next to her name."

"Hey, there's no Minnie in our class!" said Bobby.

"Minnie's for Minnie Mouse," I explained.

"She's not in our class either," said Bobby.

"Ms. Thompson's using her name as an example," I said.

"Smartypants," said Bobby.

"Listen, boys and girls," said Ms. Thompson. She waited for us to get quiet. "Our ballot will be secret. No one will know who you vote for. The student with the most votes wins."

Right then and there, I knew I didn't want to be president. Making a speech made me nervous, and you had to be good at art to make posters and flyers. No one would vote for me anyway, except my one and only friend, Peter Cavelli. They'd all vote for Lisa, the prettiest, most popular girl in class. No, not me. I have straight brown hair that sticks out of my hair bands, a million freckles, and glasses that stay smudgy no matter how many times I wipe them with my fingers.

Nope, getting nominated for class president was definitely not a good idea.

CHAPTER 2

SURPRISE

The following Monday, I sat at my desk staring out the window. Suddenly, I heard Ms. Thompson call my name, "Samantha! You've been nominated."

At first I thought I was hearing things, but then she looked me right in the eye and said, "Stand here, next to Lisa." She pointed to a spot at the front of the class.

Oh no, how could that be? Someone had nominated me for class president! Who would do a thing like that?

I wanted to disappear fast, like my hamster

does when I let him out of his cage. I planted my feet on the floor and slumped down in my chair.

"I think there's some mistake," I mumbled.

"Someone nominated you, Samantha," Ms. Thompson said, smiling.

I shook my head. "I don't think so. It must be a different Samantha."

Bobby snickered. He stood in front of the class next to Lisa. He'd been nominated too. I bet Tommy Tagaloney picked him.

"There's only one Samantha in this class," Ms. Thompson said. She showed me the paper she was holding. "See, here's your name."

The letters were kind of squiggly and some didn't stay in the lines like they were supposed to, but you could still read it. It said, "Samantha Pojanowski."

Ms. Thompson kept looking at me. I knew I had to get up and stand in front of the class. I didn't want to because up there, everybody stares at you. I tried to think of a way out. Maybe I could ask to go to the bathroom.

"Come Samantha," she said, with a stern look in her eye. So much for the bathroom idea.

I shuffled up and stood behind Lisa. I kept my head down, and studied my shoes.

After that, there were no more nominations.

Peter Cavelli raised his hand.

"Yes, Peter?" asked Ms. Thompson.

"Can they have campaign managers?" he asked. He stared at me and smiled.

"Hmmm," she said. "I hadn't thought of that. Well, I certainly see no harm in it."

She wrote the words, "CAMPAIGN MANAGER" on the board. "A campaign manager is someone who helps you with your posters, flyers, and speech. Bobby, Lisa and Samantha, you may each pick someone."

"Deena!" said Lisa. Deena looked around the class and glowed like a light-up yo-yo.

"Tommy!" said Bobby. Tommy turned to the boys and made a fist.

"Samantha?" she asked.

Peter's ears perked up, like my cousin's dog when he hears someone at the door.

"I don't know," I mumbled.

Peter sighed. His eyes drooped. That's when I knew Peter must have nominated me.

I decided to make him my campaign manager, but I didn't want to say his name out loud. Girls didn't pick boys in third grade. If I did, Lisa and Deena would probably make fun of us. Once, Lisa called us lovebirds just because we ate lunch together in the cafeteria. Maybe I could whisper Peter's name in Ms. Thompson's ear.

Before I got there, Ms. Thompson said, "Well, Samantha, you can decide later. Tomorrow, the three of you may bring in a poster."

"Now," she said to the class. "Please take out your science books."

And that's the story of how I got nominated, just like that, and I couldn't do a thing about it.

CHAPTER 3

THE CAMPAIGN TRAIL

When I got home from school, my mom asked about my day.

"I got nominated for class president," I said. "Only I don't want to be president."

"Why not?" she said. "It's an honor to be nominated."

"Because you have to make a speech in front of the whole class, and make flyers and posters, which I'm not good at. Then, you have to come up with new ideas, but I don't have any. Everybody's going to vote for Lisa Logan anyway."

My mom frowned at me.

"I'm sure you can think of something. Why don't you write down some ideas? Then we'll go to the store and pick up poster board and markers."

I shrugged. "I guess."

After snack, I ran upstairs and sat at my desk. I took out paper and sharpened my pencil. The blank page just sat there.

Ms. Thompson was a good teacher. There just wasn't anything to fix in her class. I thought about my other classes, like art, computers, and library.

Mrs. Bookbinder was our librarian. The library was my favorite place in the whole school. All those books to read. There were so many that if I spent all day in the library, every day of the year, I'd never finish them.

That's when I figured out an idea. What if we could have more library time? Instead of once a week, we could go twice or three times, maybe even every day. We could pick out more books and spend hours reading. That would be a good change.

I started writing. When I was done, I read the words out loud. I thought it sounded good.

Maybe running for president wasn't so hard after all. I zoomed through my homework. Then my mom and I went to the store for poster board and markers.

When we got home, she asked, "Do you need help?"

"Nope, I can do it myself."

My mom looked disappointed.

I ran upstairs with my supplies. I drew a big open book with the words on the pages. This is what it looked like:

When I was done, I took one last look. The poster looked good so I rolled it up. I slid on a rubber band and twisted it twice to make it tight. I placed it by my backpack.

My mom and dad asked to see it, but I didn't show them. Instead, I thought about coming home on Friday and surprising them with the good news. Samantha Pojanowski, the new class president.

CHAPTER 4

PROMISES

Tuesday morning, I brought my poster to school. It was a warm November morning. Deena and Stacey Spiros stood by the fence, talking.

"Lisa thinks you have the coolest clothes in class," Deena said. "Vote for Lisa and she'll invite you to her sleepover party Saturday."

"Thanks," said Stacey, beaming. "I will."

Great, I thought. Deena's inviting girls to Lisa's party just to get votes. I dropped my head and walked away. I almost bumped into Tommy. He was talking to Mark Klein.

"Hey Mark, you want to play football at the

park this Saturday with me and Bobby?"

"Yeah," said Mark.

"Vote for Bobby for president, and he'll make you quarterback," Tommy said.

"Awesome!" said Mark.

I slipped away.

All the girls were going to vote for Lisa and the boys were going to vote for Bobby. I looked at my poster. Maybe it wasn't such a good poster after all.

Just then, someone tapped me on the shoulder.

"Hi Samantha." It was Peter. "Can I see your poster?"

"I don't know," I said.

"Well, can you tell me what it says? Please."

"Okay, I guess." I whispered in his ear.

"Hmmm," he said. "That's a good idea Samantha, but..."

"But what?" I asked.

"But…" Peter looked at his shoes and

squirmed.

Maybe Peter didn't like my poster idea. I shouldn't have told him. Good thing I hadn't made him my campaign manager. I glared at him.

Peter saw my face, and shrugged. "Hey, how about if I help you make flyers?"

"Oh," I said. Hmmm. I could use help.

Then his face lit up and he added, "I can help you with your speech, too."

Maybe he should be my campaign manager.

"Peter," I said. "Do you want to be…"

Just then, the whistle blew and we lined up. Ms. Thompson came over and told everyone to be quiet. There was no more time to talk to Peter.

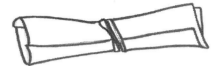

CHAPTER 5

POSTER PROBLEMS

"Do you have your posters?" asked Ms. Thompson.

"Yes," said Lisa and Bobby.

When Ms. Thompson looked at me, I nodded

"Okay Bobby, why don't you go first."

Bobby motioned for Tommy to join him. They walked to the front of the classroom and unrolled the poster.

Three big magazine pictures were glued to the poster. One man was playing football, another basketball, and the third, baseball. On top, in big block letters, it said:

BE ON THE WINNING TEAM
VOTE FOR BOBBY

Some boys shouted, "Ooh, awesome."

"Hey, that's Manny Downing running for a touchdown," shouted Kevin McCann.

"That's Jordan Swoosh making a basket," said Mark Klein.

"That's Erik Speeder hitting a homerun, " said Kevin.

"Go Bobby!"

Ms. Thompson told everybody to be quiet.

"Nice job," she said.

I bet Bobby's parents helped him make that poster. Maybe they even did the whole thing. Bobby didn't write that neatly in class.

Then it was Lisa's turn. Deena walked up with her. They unrolled her poster.

There were pictures of TV stars, and singers in cool outfits. They had been cut from magazines, too. On the top, in fancy letters, it said:

Vote for Lisa
She's Got Style

"Wow, it's Sasha & Haley from the movies," said Stacey Spiros.

"It's Zoe from TV," said Jenny Becker.

"It's Selena from Star Power," said Stacey.

"They look awesome!"

"Okay, Lisa," said Ms. Thompson. Then she looked at me.

Lisa's parents had helped her, too. Maybe I should have asked my mom for help. Oh well, too late now. I had no choice but to go up there.

I took a deep breath. Peter started waving his arms around. It looked like he wanted to join me. I shook my head. He wasn't my campaign manager yet.

I shuffled up front. My knees shook and my hands sweated. I peeked at the class.

The kids reminded me of this magazine picture I saw once. There was a hawk with big wide wings and a sharp curved beak flying over a scared little rabbit. You could tell the hawk wanted to eat the rabbit. I felt just like the rabbit.

I started to slide the rubber band off my poster. It only moved up a little because it was so tight. I kept working at it. When it got to the top, I pushed hard. The rubber band flew off like a rocket and disappeared. Before I could take a single breath, I felt a little plop on top of my head.

The kids giggled. I froze.

Ms. Thompson came over and plucked the rubber band off my head and dropped it on her desk.

"Okay class," she said. "That's enough. Let's give Samantha our attention."

I unrolled my poster. It was so wide that I had to stretch my hands all the way behind me to hold it. It covered my entire body.

The giggles got louder.

"Shhh," Ms. Thompson said. She made a spinning motion with her hands.

I wondered why.

She spun her hands again.

I turned myself around in a circle.

The class laughed.

"No, Samantha," she said. "It's your poster. It's backwards. Turn it around."

I looked down. Sure enough, the blank side faced the class. My face got hot like the time I had a sore throat and a fever of 104.

I tried to turn the poster around but it snapped back into a tight circle. More laughs.

"Shhh," said Ms. Thompson again.

I turned the poster around and then tried unrolling it. Finally, I got it open and made sure that the blank side faced my body.

Bobby laughed so hard, he fell out of his seat.

Ms. Thompson yelled at him. Then she came

over and whispered in my ear.

"It's upside down," she said.

I felt so horrible, I just lifted the poster and covered my face. Ms. Thompson slid it out of my hands. She turned it around and held it up.

At first, the kids got quiet. Then Lisa kind of rolled her eyes up.

Ms. Thompson said, "Great idea, Samantha," and gave Lisa a DON'T EVEN THINK ABOUT IT look. She asked me to sit down.

I heard Lisa whisper to Deena, "It figures Samantha Smartypants would come up with a geeky idea like that."

"Yeah," said Deena. "Better for us. Now for sure, she won't get any votes."

That was the final straw. Not the kind you drink chocolate milk with. What I mean is, I couldn't stand it anymore.

I decided to quit. Then all my problems would be over.

I felt better but then my dad's face flashed before my eyes. He said, "There are no quitters in our family." Hmmm. Now what?

My dad's voice kept talking. "When the going gets tough, the tough get going."

Well, I certainly wanted to get going. Right to bed and never come out. But that's not what he meant. He meant I had to stick with it. It was Tuesday. The election was Friday. A billion years away!

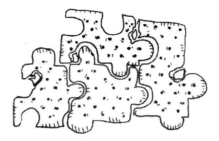

CHAPTER 6

SNACK PLANS

"Don't forget to bring in a snack tomorrow," Deena told Lisa, while lining up to go home. "That way you'll get more votes."

"Did you hear that?" Tommy asked Bobby. "Lisa's bringing snacks to get votes. You better bring one too."

Peter turned to me and raised his eyebrows. I could tell he wanted me to do the same. I wanted to ask him what to bring and make him my campaign manager, but just then, my mom showed up. She asked me how the poster worked out.

"I don't want to talk about it," I said.

"Oh, sweetie. " She gave me one of those I'M

SURE IT WORKED OUT FINE looks.

Moms don't always know everything.

I stayed quiet in the car. At home, my mom made me a snack of my favorite whole wheat crackers, Swiss cheese, and an apple.

She didn't like junk food. At Back to School Night, the nurse talked about kids eating too much sugar and fat. Since then, my mom fed me healthy snacks. I didn't mind though, because the crackers tasted good, and I liked the holes in the cheese.

After snack, I ran upstairs and did my homework. Then, I wrote down all the kids' names in class and counted them. Twenty-four plus Ms. Thompson. I needed a snack for twenty-five.

I rushed downstairs to the kitchen. My mom called from around the corner in her office.

"Still hungry, Samantha? Do you want me to make you something?"

"Nope," I said. "I'll do it myself."

"The bananas are ripe," she said.

"Okay."

The box of whole wheat crackers was still on the counter. I tipped it over and counted the crackers. There were eighteen whole crackers and a bunch of broken ones. Not enough! I moved the broken pieces together in one spot. They looked like pieces of a jigsaw puzzle. That gave me an idea. I fit them together to make seven more crackers. Now I had enough! If only I could make them stick together.

Glue wouldn't work because it would make the kids sick. I checked inside a cabinet. A bag of flour caught my eye. That was it. Our second grade teacher taught us how to make paste from flour and water.

In a bowl, I mixed up a scoop of flour and some water. I looked at the paste. Oh, no, I thought. The crackers were brown but the paste was white. How could I make it brown? I got an idea.

In art class, we'd learned that mixing red, yellow, and blue makes brown. I needed to find the food coloring that my mom used. Hmm.

My mom kept spices on a little round platter in a cabinet. She called it a Lazy Susan. I'm not sure who Susan is, and calling someone lazy isn't very nice. Anyway, you can spin the platter around and find what you want without taking everything out.

I spun the platter round and round. It was so much fun, I kept on spinning. Faster and faster. It got so fast, that all the spices flew off the platter. Crash! Some of them landed on the floor.

"Are you okay?" called out my mom.

"Fine," I said. "I dropped something but it didn't break."

"Are you sure?" she asked. I thought I heard her getting up.

"Yep, really sure," I said, quickly. I held my breath until I heard her slump back down.

I picked up spice bottles until I found the food coloring. I added three drops of blue to the bowl of flour and water and mixed, then three drops of yellow. It turned green. I just needed to add the red drops to make brown. I turned the red bottle upside down, but nothing came out. Oh no, it was empty. All I had was green goop.

Then I remembered a book by Dr. Seuss about green eggs and ham. Maybe the kids would like green crackers too.

I plunged my finger in and took a gob of green paste. I rubbed it on the broken cracker pieces and stuck them together. At first, they didn't stay, so I had to use more goop.

When I was done, I looked at the crackers. They looked pretty. I stacked them on a plate, brought them upstairs to my room and placed them by the heating vent to dry.

When I skipped back downstairs, I thought about Bobby and Lisa. What if their snack was better? That's when I decided to bring in two snacks.

I dashed over to the refrigerator and searched. Nothing but milk, juice, and leftovers. Finally, in the bottom drawer, I spotted a bag of carrots and a box of cherry tomatoes. The carrot bag looked half empty, but the box of tomatoes was full.

I spilled all the tomatoes onto the counter. Some of them rolled right off and scooted away. No matter how hard I looked, I couldn't find them. Oh well. It looked like there were still plenty left. I counted. Twenty-five! Yeah!

I put them in a zip-lock bag and brought them to my room. I set them down next to the crackers. Maybe the kids would vote for me after all.

When I came downstairs, my mom stood in the middle of the kitchen with one hand on her forehead and her eyes about to pop.

"YIKES!" she yelled. "What happened?"

I looked around. There were cracker crumbs

and spices on the floor. Food coloring, and flour covered the countertop. A spoon full of green muck stuck to the mixing bowl. In the corner, I saw two flattened cherry tomatoes with squishy seeds splattered around. So that's where they went.

"Uh, oh."

My mom made me clean up. She wanted to know what I'd been doing.

"Top secret," I said.

She gave me a funny look but I didn't tell.

"I don't know, Samantha." My mom turned on the vacuum cleaner.

That night, I dreamt about school. In the dream, I won the election. The kids clapped and Ms. Thompson said, "Congratulations!" I looked at her and gasped. She had a carrot stuck up her nose, two cherry tomato eyes, and a big goopy green mustache.

CHAPTER 7

SNACK DELIVERY

Wednesday, I woke early. I grabbed the plate of crackers and the bag of tomatoes from my bedroom floor. Then I snuck downstairs. It was still dark. My eyes kept sucking shut like they were attached to the vacuum cleaner.

I put the crackers into a zip-lock bag. Then I put the two zip-lock bags into a grocery bag and put them in my backpack.

Later that morning in the schoolyard, I heard Deena talking to Jenny.

"Lisa thinks you have the coolest clothes in

class. Vote for her and she'll invite you to her sleepover."

"Thanks," said Jenny, beaming. "I will."

Oh no, not again.

I snuck over to the other side of the yard. Tommy was talking to Kevin.

"Hey Kevin, you want to play football this Saturday with me and Bobby?"

"Oh yeah."

"Vote for Bobby and he'll make you quarterback."

"Cool!"

I walked away.

When our class arrived at Ms. Thompson's room, Lisa and Deena marched straight to the teacher's desk. They carried a big platter of fudge brownies. Each one was covered in plastic wrap, with a toothpick flag that said, "Vote for Lisa!" They were so perfect, you could tell Lisa's mom had made them.

"I brought these for the class," said Lisa, smiling.

"Everybody loves brownies," added Deena.

"Okay," said Ms. Thompson, taking the platter and setting it on a shelf. "You can pass them out after lunch."

"Hey," said Bobby, running to the desk with a shopping bag. "I've got a snack, too!"

Bobby reached inside and pulled out packs of potato chips. Mrs. Stanger must have spent a lot of money on all those chips. Ms. Thompson put the chips next to the brownies

Maybe I should have asked my mom for help, too. But, then I remembered I had two snacks instead of just one.

I took out my grocery bag and tried to slide past Lisa and Deena on my way to Ms. Thompson's desk. I couldn't get by.

"Hey, what's in the bag?" Lisa asked. She reached over to snatch it out of my hand. I didn't want her to ruin my surprise so I shoved the bag under my shirt and held it tight. Something went squish, but I didn't let go.

"Ooh, gross," yelled Bobby.

"Quiet," said Ms. Thompson. She held her hand out. I gave her the bag and she placed it next to the other snacks.

Phew, my secret's safe, I thought. I turned my head to Peter and grinned.

CHAPTER 8

SLICK SLOGANS

When everybody settled down, Ms. Thompson wrote a big word on the board, "SLOGAN."

"Today, we're going to talk about slogans. A slogan is a catchy saying that people remember. You can use it in a campaign to get people to vote for you. Sometimes, slogans rhyme."

She told us about a man named Eisenhower who ran for president and used a slogan. Ms. Thompson wrote it on the board:

I LIKE IKE

"Ike is Mr. Eisenhower's nickname."

"I'd use a nickname too, if my name was Eyes

and Hower," said Bobby. Tommy laughed.

Then Ms. Thompson taught us about William Harrison who ran for president. His slogan was, "Tippecanoe and Tyler Too."

"A man who tips over a canoe is too clumsy to be president!" said Lisa.

Ms. Thompson grinned. "Does anyone know what this slogan means?"

I raised my hand.

"Yes, Samantha?"

"Mr. Harrison won a battle at a place called Tippecanoe, and Tyler is his vice president's name." My dad taught me that. He loved history and so did I.

"Excellent," said Ms. Thompson. "You're right."

"Samantha Smartypants," whispered Lisa.

I ignored her.

After that, Ms. Thompson told Bobby, Lisa and me that we could each make a flyer with a slogan for the election. During free reading time, we'd use the classroom computers. She'd make copies to hand out. It sounded like fun.

When it was time, Lisa, Deena, Bobby, and Tommy dashed to the back of the room. From the corner of my eye, I saw Peter waving his arms. I wanted him to help me with my flyer, but he still wasn't my campaign manager. I shrugged and walked to the last computer.

Mrs. Bittle, our computer teacher, had shown us what to do. I clicked twice and looked at the new blank page that came up. Then I thought about my slogan. What could I use?

My snacks popped into my head. Bobby's and Lisa's snacks had lots of sugar and fat. Mine were healthy. I thought of a rhyme:

HEALTHY FOOD AND LOTS OF REST HELP YOU PASS YOUR SPELLING TEST! VOTE SAMANTHA, THE HEALTHY CHOICE!

It sounded great.

"Do you need any help, Samantha?" Ms. Thompson asked, walking over.

I covered the screen with my arms and shook my head. She moved over to help Bobby and Lisa.

On my screen, I changed the letters to make them look cool. I clicked on "Images" and found some pictures of carrots and brussel sprouts. I didn't want to use tomatoes and crackers, because they would ruin my surprise.

When I finished, I raised my hand. Ms. Thompson looked up from Lisa's computer. "Yes, Samantha?"

"I'm all done."

"Okay. Go ahead and send it to the printer."

I clicked the printer button on my screen, and ran to get my flyer before anybody saw it.

I glanced over at Peter. His head was buried in a book. When he looked up, I gave him a thumbs-up.

CHAPTER 9

MY CAMPAIGN MANAGER

At lunch, Peter sat at my table. We took out sandwiches, drinks, and fruit. Nobody sat next to us.

"Peter," I whispered. "Would you like to be my campaign manager?"

His eyes lit up. "Yes. I would. I have some really good ideas too."

"Great," I said. "You can help me with my speech."

"Why don't you come to my house after school and we'll work on it," he said.

"I'll ask my mom when she picks me up."

"Okay." He took a bite of his sandwich. Then he looked up at me and asked, "So what does your flyer say, anyway?"

"You'll see." I thought Peter would like my flyer because he ate healthy food too.

After lunch, I walked up to Ms. Thompson.

"I made Peter my campaign manager," I whispered in her ear, looking around for eavesdroppers.

"I can't hear you Samantha. Did you say Peter's in pain?"

I whispered louder, taking a breath in between each word, "Nooo, I – made – Pee…."

"In your pants?" she asked. "You had an accident?"

"NO," I yelled. "I MADE PETER MY CAMPAIGN MANAGER!"

Kids turned around and stared. Now the cat was out of the bag. Which doesn't mean I brought a pet to school and it escaped. Now everybody knew I'd picked Peter to be my campaign manager. Peter smiled, but Lisa and Deena just shook their heads.

"Good idea," said Ms. Thompson.

"It figures," said Lisa to Deena. "I think they're in love."

CHAPTER 10

SLIME

Ms. Thompson picked up three stacks of paper from her desk. She handed Lisa, Bobby, and me a set.

"Ask your campaign managers to hand these out while you pass around your snacks," she said.

I gave my flyers to Peter. He glanced at them, and raised his eyebrows. I walked over to the shelf to get my bag.

Lisa and Bobby got there first. They handed out their snacks. Some kids whistled and said, "Awesome!"

I picked up my grocery bag and reached inside.

My fingers touched something wet and slimy. Yuck! I pulled my hand out fast and lifted it up. Goopy red liquid and seeds trickled down my fingers, covering my sleeve.

Oh no, I thought. What happened?

I took the bag and dumped it out on Ms. Thompson's desk.

"Samantha!" she yelled, grabbing her papers and books away.

The zip-lock bag had opened up and squished-up tomatoes splattered all over the desk. Ms. Thompson gasped. She grabbed her pencil box and water bottle. Then she yelled, "Samantha, quick, get paper towels!"

I ran to the back of the room. When I got to the paper towel holder, I pulled on the brown sheet hard. The paper ripped. I threw it on the ground and pulled out another one. It ripped too.

"Hurry, Samantha," said Ms. Thompson. I looked back. She had her hand cupped on the side of her desk, catching red drippings.

I pulled again. The paper towel didn't rip. Hooray! I ran back to Ms. Thompson's desk. She looked at the mess on her desk. Then, she looked at the one towel in my hand.

"Samantha," she said. "I need more than one, please."

She was right. One towel wasn't enough. I dropped it in the garbage. She sighed.

"Oops," I said, and dropped my head.

On the floor, the puddle of thick reddish liquid grew.

"Hurry," said Ms. Thompson.

I ran. Then the worst thing in the world happened. My sneaker slid in the red slimy stuff and I landed right on my butt. It only hurt a little but when I touched my pants, they felt wet. Ms. Thompson helped me get up.

"Are you okay?" she asked.

I nodded and tiptoed back to the paper towels.

I heard giggles but kept going. It was important to get Ms. Thompson's towels. Lisa Logan beat me to it.

I turned around. Bobby was pointing at me.

"Samantha wet her pants," he said.

I bet my face turned redder than the squished-up tomatoes.

"Be quiet," ordered Ms. Thompson.

Lisa rushed up to her.

"Here's your towels," she said, beaming. She handed them to Ms. Thompson.

I shuffled to the front of the room, careful to walk around the mess on the floor. Ms. Thompson cleaned her desk, while Lisa and I wiped the floor. We threw the soaking towels in the garbage.

When I looked up, Ms. Thompson had my bag of crackers hanging between her thumb and forefinger.

"These look okay, I think," she said. "Why don't you hand them out?"

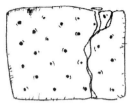

CHAPTER 11

CRACKER CRISIS

I took the bag, opened it, and walked around placing a cracker on each desk. Most of the kids said they didn't want any. Peter said, "I'll take two," without even looking.

Bobby, Tommy, Lisa and Deena were still handing out flyers and treats. I grabbed some crackers, and placed one on each of their desks.

When I returned to my seat, I found a brownie and chips with flyers underneath. I sat down. My pants felt wet and sticky. I lifted up the snacks and looked at the flyers. This is what Lisa's said:

Here's the coolest campaign slogan.

The best class president is Lisa Logan.

It had a picture of a cheerleader in a blue and gold costume with a pom-pom in one hand and a megaphone in the other. Inside a word bubble were the words:

Yeah Lisa!!

The girls would love Lisa's flyer. Maybe I should have let Ms. Thompson help me, too. I sunk lower in my seat.

Bobby's flyer was next. His had a picture of a scary vampire dressed in a black cape with fangs. The vampire was pointing and saying:

DO AS THE VAMPIRE SEZ
VOTE FOR BOBBY FOR CLASS PREZ
OR ELSE!!!!!

Bobby's looked scary, but I figured the boys would love it. I picked up mine. It wasn't half as cool. Not one chance in a trillion would I get any votes. I closed my eyes and tried to disappear.

All of a sudden, somebody screamed. My eyes popped open.

"There's green mold on my cracker," yelled Bobby, dangling his cracker and holding his nose.

I tried to tell him it was just food coloring but before I could say anything, Tommy, shouted, "Mine, too!"

"Eeeek!" screeched Lisa.

She swept her cracker off her desk.

"Yuck!" yelled Deena, scrunching her nose.

"Samantha tried to poison us to win the election!" Bobby said, pointing at me just like the vampire in his flyer.

I looked at Peter. He looked sorry for me. Then he picked up his half-eaten cracker and examined it closely. His face turned a sickly shade of green.

"Food coloring," I whispered, but he didn't hear me.

Ms. Thompson banged her fist on her desk.

"That's enough!" she yelled. All the kids got quiet. Ms. Thompson looked very tired. She took a deep breath and picked up the wastepaper basket. Then, she walked up and down the aisles flicking crackers off the desks into the basket.

"It's time for library," said Ms. Thompson, looking at the clock. "Please line up."

Before I stood up, she came over, leaned

down, and put her arm around me. "It's okay, Samantha. Sometimes things don't work out the way you plan. But, you're a very smart girl with lots of great ideas." Then she looked me straight in the eye. "Don't give up." She sounded just like my dad.

I felt a bit better, but not much. Running for class president had to be the hardest job in the entire galaxy.

CHAPTER 12

HELPING OTHERS

After library, we returned to the classroom.
Ms. Thompson greeted us with a kind smile. All
her books, pencils and papers were stacked neatly
on her desk. When we settled down, she spoke
with a calm, happy voice.

"The holidays are next month when many of
you will receive lots of gifts. Not everybody is as
lucky as you. Some children's families can't afford
presents. This season, our class will help one of
those families."

She picked up a photograph and brought it

around the classroom. In it, there was a mom and three boys. One looked like he was our age, and the other two were little. "This is the Jackson family," she said.

"Hey, that's my last name," said Deena.

"Mrs. Jackson lost her job," said Ms. Thompson. "We're going to help the family buy presents."

Tommy raised his hand. "How can we buy presents without any money."

"Good question, Tommy. Does anyone have an idea?"

"Sell makeup," said Lisa.

"Sell our textbooks!" yelled Bobby.

"Very funny," said Ms. Thompson. She tapped her finger on the side of her head. "Hmmm. I just thought of something. Why don't our nominees think of an idea and talk about it tomorrow in their speeches."

It sounded really hard. I looked at Peter. He

whispered, "I'll help you."

"Don't worry about memorizing," said Ms. Thompson. "You can write your speeches on index cards."

When my mom picked me up, I asked her about going to Peter's house. She talked to his mom.

"I'll pick you up at 4:30, Samantha," she told me.

"Great!" I knew Peter was really smart. Today we were going to write the best speech in the whole universe. I hoped.

CHAPTER 13

PETER'S HOUSE

We arrived at a small white house with black shutters. Inside, Mrs. Cavelli gave us granola bars and milk. Then she let us use the kitchen computer.

Peter pulled an extra chair over and we sat.

"Do you have any ideas?" I asked.

"I'm thinking," he said.

"I have an idea. How about a used book sale? We could have everybody bring in their old books and sell them for one dollar each."

"Ummm, maybe, Samantha," he said. "But not all the kids love books. We need something more popular."

"All Lisa and her friends talk about is clothes,"
I muttered.

"And Bobby's friends talk about sports," Peter
added.

"We'll need to do something for everybody."

Neither of us came up with any ideas. I think
we were trying too hard. My dad says that
sometimes you just have to relax and let the ideas
come to you.

We both stared at the computer.

"Why don't we play a game while we're
thinking," I said.

He clicked on *Game Station.* "My favorite
game is *Brain Busters,* " Peter said.

"Okay, you go first."

Peter got to Level 10 with over 18,000 points.
Then we switched seats.

"My favorite game is *Word Worm,* " I said.

"I never played that one."

I got to Level 12.

Then we switched seats again and Peter clicked back to the homepage. The screen blinked and played music.

All of a sudden, Peter shouted, "That's it, Samantha." He pointed to a game that had just flashed on the screen.

"What?"

"*Touchdown*, It's a new football game."

"So?"

"Bobby's friends will love this game."

"What's that got to do with making money?"

"Or writing a speech?" said Mrs. Cavelli, walking over. "I didn't realize you two were playing games."

"We can make money by holding a computer contest. Everybody loves computers," explained Peter. "We'll charge the kids one dollar each to play. The kids with the highest scores will win prizes."

"Wow," I said. "That's a super idea."

"Sounds great," agreed Mrs. Cavelli, walking away to start dinner.

Peter clicked on *Touchdown.* When the screen asked what player he wanted to be, he selected quarterback. He had to decide whether to throw or hand off the ball, then click on the mouse at just the right time. If he clicked too soon or too late, his teammates would drop the ball. Peter didn't get any touchdowns.

"That's okay," I said. "Bobby's friends will love this game, but what about everybody else?"

Peter clicked back to the homepage. We watched the screen while new game ads flashed by.

"There!" I pointed at one that said, *Shopping Spree.*

We switched seats. I clicked and read the Help file. I'd get $50 to shop for clothes and pick out the best outfit for my money. Then I'd model the clothes down the runway of a fashion show. If all the judges liked my outfit, I'd win a $100 prize.

With the money, I'd shop for more clothes at even more stores. The next prize was $200.

I tried it. After the first round, the judges said my colors clashed. Oh well. I knew Lisa and her friends would love playing.

Peter and I talked about the contest. We decided to give prizes for the top three scores in each game.

"We can ask Toy Barn to donate the prizes," I said.

"Great idea, Samantha," said Mrs. Cavelli, while stirring a pot at the stove.

Peter and I smiled. We had a great plan.

We spent the next half hour working on my speech. I copied it down on index cards and practiced in front of Peter and his mom. Mrs. Cavelli told me to look up, smile, and speak slowly. At the end, she and Peter clapped.

When my mom picked me up at 4:30, I told her that Peter and I had written a great speech, and

I was going to be the next class president.

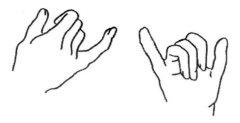

CHAPTER 14

BROKEN PROMISES

When I got to school the next day, I saw a group of girls in the yard.

"Deena told me my clothes were the coolest!" shouted Jenny. "I'm invited to Lisa's sleepover."

"She told me mine were the coolest," yelled Stacey. "And she invited me first."

More girls came over and started shouting.

Finally, Lisa's cousin lifted her hands and yelled, "Wait a minute. Lisa's not even allowed to have sleepovers. She got grounded last time when everybody stayed up until three a.m. and made a mess."

"Hey, Deena lied to us about Lisa's party!"

said Jenny.

"I'm not voting for Lisa!" said Stacey.

Better for me, I thought. I walked to the other side of the yard.

A bunch of boys huddled together.

"No way," yelled Kevin. "I'm quarterback. Tommy said so."

"He told me I'm quarterback!" Mark stuck his face right up to Kevin's.

Kevin shoved Mark away. "Wrong, I am."

They yelled and pushed until a school aide came over and broke it up.

I walked over to Peter and told him what happened. He smiled. "They're all mad at Lisa and Bobby," he said, "for breaking their campaign promises. That means they'll vote for you instead. Just give a good speech, and you'll win for sure."

I wished Peter hadn't mentioned my speech. It made me as nervous as my mom was that time she found a snake in the garage.

CHAPTER 15

SPEECH TIME

The morning crept by. We had math and science. Finally, Ms.Thompson told us to clear our desks. It was speech time.

I squirmed in my seat.

Lisa raised her hand.

"Can I go first?" she asked.

"Okay, Lisa," answered Ms. Thompson.

Lisa strutted to the front of the room. You could tell by her perfect French braids that her mom had fixed her hair. Her shirt was one of the most popular brands. She didn't even have index cards.

"We're going to have a fashion show," she said, beaming. "And we'll charge each person five dollars to come. We'll send invitations to the whole town. And, are you ready for this? The girls in this class will be the models!"

"Yay! Cool," said Deena, nodding at the other girls.

Lisa talked about all the fancy, expensive outfits the girls would wear. She kept on talking until Ms. Thompson told her that time was up.

Some of the boys booed. A few of the girls smiled until someone mentioned Lisa's broken sleepover promise.

Peter raised his hand.

"Yes, Peter," said Ms. Thompson.

"Can I ask Lisa a question?"

"Sure."

He stared Lisa right in the eye. "How are we going to pay for all those expensive outfits?"

Lisa frowned. She turned to Deena, who shrugged. Then Deena's face brightened. "I know. They can borrow your clothes, Lisa."

"No way!," Lisa yelled.

"Enough," said Ms. Thompson. "We'll work out the details later."

She turned to the class. I held my breath.

"How about you, Bobby?" she asked.

I let out my breath in a big whoosh.

Bobby froze.

"Go up there!" said Tommy.

Bobby shuffled to the front of the class and buried his head in his cards.

"To make money, we're gonna have a field goal contest. You pay five bucks to kick the ball from the thirty-yard line. If you get it in, you win a prize. If you don't, you lose."

"Yuck," said Deena.

"I'm not paying five bucks just to kick a football," said Mark.

"Who's going to be quarterback Bobby?" said Kevin.

"Shhh!" said Ms. Thompson. "Is that all, Bobby?"

"Yep."

"Thank you." She looked at me. "Samantha?"

I turned to Peter for help. He whispered, "You can do it!"

I picked up my index cards and removed the rubber band slowly. It didn't fly off. Whew. That was a good start.

When I got to the front of the room, my hands shook like jello. My knees wobbled and my mouth felt like sandpaper. The words on my index cards went blurry.

Take a deep breath, I told myself. Look up and smile. Just like Peter's mom had taught me.

"My idea to make money is …"

"Louder please, Samantha," said Ms. Thompson. "We can't hear you."

"MY IDEA TO MAKE MONEY IS…"

"Not quite that loud."

I was about to start again when all of a sudden, I had to go. To the bathroom, I mean. Not now, I thought. I'd have to hold it in and finish my speech.

I crossed my legs. Where was I? I looked down at my cards. They shook like an earthquake. My stomach hurt. I really had to go. I squeezed my legs tight.

"My idea to make money is to have a…" That's when the worst thing in the world happened. My hands shook so hard the cards slipped right out. They landed in a jumble on the floor.

I bent down to get them. I couldn't reach because my legs were crossed. I uncrossed them, scooped up the cards, and crossed them again. Now I had to go so bad, I could barely hold it in. I shifted from side to side.

"Look, she's doing the pee-pee dance," Lisa

said to Deena.

Ms. Thompson came over and whispered in my ear.

"Why don't you go to the bathroom and come back after to finish your speech."

No way. I had to be a trooper. That's when you finish no matter what happens. I shook my head.

"Are you sure?" she asked.

"Yes, I'm sure."

I looked down at my cards and blurted out, "And that's the way we can make money and buy the family presents."

Oh, oh. That was the end of my speech. I studied the card in my hand. It was the last one instead of the first one! They had gotten mixed up when I dropped them. I shuffled and searched.

None of the cards made any sense. It was no use. The words kept running together like water in a stream. That made me have to go even worse. My head got woozy and I hunched over.

Ms. Thompson rushed to my side. She took the cards away and put her arm around my back. Then she walked me out the classroom door.

"Samantha," she said in a gentle voice. "Go to the bathroom. When you come back, you can finish your speech. I'll have Peter fix the cards for you."

Tears rolled down my face. "No way," I said. "I can't do it. Not in a quadrillion years. It's just too hard. I never wanted to be president anyway. If Peter hadn't nominated me, none of this would have happened."

I rushed down the hall to the bathroom. Lucky for me, I got there just in the nick of time.

CHAPTER 16

RESCUE

I took my time going back to the classroom. I opened the door slowly, not making a peep.

Peter stood at the front of the class holding my index cards.

"The kids with the most points in each game win prizes from Toy Barn," he said. Peter was giving my speech.

Tommy yelled out, "Awesome!" Bobby gave him a dirty look. "Oops," said Tommy.

Mark asked, "When can we start?"

Peter looked up and spotted me at the door.

"Vote for Samantha and find out. If you want a

computer contest and an awesome president, vote for Samantha!" He pointed to me. Everyone turned around and stared.

My face heated up like the burners on my mom's electric stove. To my surprise, some kids started clapping. A few of the boys even whistled.

"Samantha for President!" shouted Stacey.

"Yeah! Samantha for President!"

Lisa's and Deena's eyebrows rose so high, they disappeared into their hair. Bobby's and Tommy's mouths dropped open wide enough to fit in the globe by Ms. Thompson's desk.

Ms. Thompson looked at me and grinned.

"Okay, boys and girls. Take some time to think about your choices. Tomorrow you'll all get to vote."

Later that day, Peter brought a pencil and a notebook to lunch. We sat down at our usual table. To our surprise, a group of kids came over.

"Anybody sitting here?" asked Stacey.

"Nope," I said, almost choking on my sandwich.

The kids sat down. They asked us about the computer contest. Peter and I answered their questions. Then we talked about different computer games the kids liked. It turned out not everybody liked sports or fashion games. They suggested *Music Mania*, *Space Mission*, and someone even wanted to play *Word Worm*! The time flew by and before I knew it, we were walking to the schoolyard together for recess.

"I've got something to do," said Peter, twirling his pencil in one hand and holding the notebook in another. He walked away and marched up to a group of boys. I could see him talking, but it was too far to hear. He wrote something in his notebook. What was he up to? I had to stop watching because some girls came over and blocked my view.

"Do you want to play Red Rover?" asked

Jenny. I turned behind me to see who she was talking to. Nobody. That's when I realized she was asking me!

I played Red Rover with girls from my class. It was fun, even though I never broke through a line.

Back at the classroom, I asked Peter what he'd been doing. He showed me his notebook. There were three columns and lines like sticks. This is what it looked like:

SAMANTHA	LISA	BOBBY
‖‖ ‖‖ ‖‖ ‖‖	| |	| |

What's this?" I asked.

"It's a poll," he said.

"You mean you asked the kids who they were going to vote for?"

"Yep," he smiled.

I could see that twenty kids were going to vote for me, two for Lisa, and two for Bobby.

"You'll win by a landslide," said Peter, grinning.

It sounded like dirt falling down a mountain.

"Is that a good thing?" I asked.

"That means you'll win by lots of votes," he said.

"Oh." It was hard to believe. I didn't know what to say, except, "Thank you, Peter."

I barely paid attention the rest of the day. It felt like I was floating in a cotton candy sky. I didn't even care that cotton candy had too much sugar.

CHAPTER 17

OVERNIGHT PLANS

After school, I told my mom what happened.

"It sounds like you might be the next president," she said. "I'm proud of you whether you win or not."

My dad came home from work and gave me a big hug. I think it was the best day in my entire life. I was so glad the campaign was over, especially the speech part.

I thought about the computer contest. There was so much to do. I'd need Peter's help. If he hadn't helped me campaign, I wouldn't be getting any votes. The contest was his idea. What could I do to thank him?

I talked it over with my dad. We talked for a very long time.

When I went to sleep, I tossed and turned. My mind kept racing. Not around the room or anything. It just meant I couldn't stop thinking.

Suddenly, I turned on the light and jumped out of bed. At my desk, I started writing. When I was done, I stuck the paper in my backpack and went to lie down. Before long, I drifted off to sleep.

CHAPTER 18

ELECTION DAY

The next morning, I asked my mom to drive me to school early. I walked into the classroom and showed Ms. Thompson my paper.

"I want to hand this out," I said.

Ms. Thompson read it. "Are you sure?"

"Absolutely sure."

"Okay, let's go to the office. I'll make copies."

We brought the papers back to class. She helped me fold each page so the words faced inside. I placed one on each desk, except I left out Lisa, Deena, Bobby, Tommy, Peter and me. Then, I joined the other kids in the schoolyard. When the whistle blew, we lined up.

Kids whispered about the election. Stacey even pointed to me and smiled. Lisa looked worried.

"I'm sure you'll win, Lisa," Deena told her.

Lisa gave me a sideways look.

Tommy reassured Bobby. "Don't worry, none of the boys will vote for a girl."

Back in the classroom, everybody put away their jackets and sat down.

"What's this?" asked Stacey, picking up the paper on her desk.

"I don't know," said Jenny, looking at hers. "Let's open it."

Peter looked at his desk and then at mine.

"What's going on?" he asked. "How come we didn't get anything?"

I shrugged and hid my face.

Papers rustled as kids read. Stacey and Jenny turned to look at me. I nodded. They turned to Peter. He checked his nose for boogers, and fixed his glasses.

Lisa tried to peek at everybody's desk, but the kids just covered their papers with their arms. Tommy and Bobby frowned. I got so nervous that I forgot to breathe.

Finally, Ms. Thompson announced, "Okay boys and girls, it's time to vote."

She handed out ballots with the names, "Samantha", "Lisa", and "Bobby" on them.

"Check off the box next to the person you're voting for. Then turn over your ballot and raise your hand. I'll collect them. Please read a book while I count the votes."

The kids started writing. Hands shot up and Ms. Thompson walked over to pick up the ballots. Then she returned to her desk and started counting.

Everybody kept sneaking peeks at her. Lisa walked over and asked to go to the bathroom.

"Not now," said Ms. Thompson.

Bobby craned his neck out so far I thought it

would pop off. When Ms. Thompson saw him, he buried his face in his book. He didn't even notice that the book was upside down.

It took a zillion hours. I couldn't concentrate. I wanted to know who won. It felt worse than waiting on line for Space Mountain at Disney World.

Finally, Ms. Thompson announced, "We have a tie. Two students got the same amount of votes. So, instead of one class president, we're going to have two. They're called co-presidents. The two students are…" She looked at Lisa, then at Bobby. When she turned to me, she smiled.

"Samantha Pojanowski and… Peter Cavelli!"

"Hooray," yelled Stacey and Kevin.

"What?" shouted Bobby.

Hmm, I thought. Kids must have really wanted me to be president.

Peter did one of those double-takes, like Ms. Thompson did back in September when Bobby stuck a piece of gum on her eraser.

Lisa's hand shot up.

"Yes?" asked Ms. Thompson.

"There must be some mistake. Peter didn't run for President."

"Right," said Bobby. "He cheated!"

"Actually," Ms. Thompson said, "Peter won by a write-in vote."

"What's that?" asked Deena.

"That's when you write the name of somebody you want to win on your ballot, even though they're not listed."

"That's illegal!" yelled Tommy.

"Actually not. Peter got ten write-in votes and Samantha got ten regular votes. They're our new class presidents."

Peter looked at me. "How did that happen?" he whispered, tapping his pencil on his desk.

I grinned. "I guess you're just really popular!" I said.

CHAPTER 19

THE COMPUTER CONTEST

For the next two weeks, Ms. Thompson worked with me, Peter, and the class planning the computer contest. Ms. Thompson suggested I ask Lisa and her friends to make posters. That's when they stopped acting so mad. I asked Bobby and Tommy to help run the sports games. The computer teacher, Mrs. Bittle, set up the laptops, and my mom drove us to Toy Barn to get prizes.

After awhile, Peter and I got used to being co-presidents.

"It's not that hard," I said. "Once you get

everybody to help."

On the day of the contest, the whole school buzzed with excitement. Kids lined up for miles, each paying a dollar to play. We made $197, enough money to buy everything on the Jackson family's wish list, and some extra surprises too.

The class wrapped the presents. Bobby and Tommy made sure to wrap the brand new football. Lisa and Deena wrapped Mrs. Jackson's new sweater. Then Ms. Thompson surprised us all.

"Instead of delivering the presents to the Jacksons, we're going to give them to the family here. I've invited them to our holiday party."

"We'll need treats for the party," said Peter.

"I'll bring my brownies," said Lisa.

"And I'll bring chips," added Bobby.

Three more kids volunteered to bring snacks. To my surprise, one of them was me. The class groaned.

"Are you sure, Samantha?" asked Ms.

Thompson, wrinkling her forehead.

"Yes," I answered, with a big, loud voice. I had an idea.

"Uh, oh," said Lisa.

I talked over my idea with my mom. Then we invited Peter over to help us make the treats. We had a great time.

The day of the party, I brought a big tray covered with foil up to Ms. Thompson's desk.

"Put it over there," she said nervously, covering her desk with her arms.

I set them on the shelf. All morning, Ms. Thompson kept peeking at my tray. I think she was checking for leaks.

When the Jackson family showed up in our classroom after lunch, everybody cheered. The two younger boys, Will and Marcus jumped up and down when they unwrapped their action figures and remote control cars. Derrick, who was our age, tossed his football up in the air and tried on his brand new sneakers. Mrs. Jackson modeled her new sweater.

Then it was time for treats. The volunteers rushed to hand them out. I went last and grabbed my tray. A big hush fell over the room. Ms. Thompson held her breath. I lifted the foil and showed the class.

There were thirty giant, perfectly shaped, chocolate covered strawberries with a colorful toothpick stuck in each one.

"Oooh," chanted Mrs. Jackson. "I love chocolate covered strawberries."

"Me too," said Ms. Thompson, letting out her breath.

"Over here," Will, Marcus, and Derrick shouted, as I handed them out.

Everybody took one. They were the most popular treat of the party.

Later, the three boys skipped out of the class with their mother carrying shopping bags full of gifts. The whole class smiled along with Ms. Thompson.

Peter walked over to me. "The chocolate covered strawberries were a hit, Samantha," he said, grinning.

"And strawberries and dark chocolate keep everybody healthy, too," I reminded him.

"Right," said Peter. We both laughed.

Then Peter got all serious. "So, Samantha, it's time you told me your big secret. How did I get so many write-in votes on election day?"

"Oh," I said, wondering whether to tell him. I decided to spill the beans. Which doesn't mean I dropped food on the floor. I just decided to tell Peter the truth. I walked over to my desk, pulled out a crumpled piece of paper, and gave it to Peter. He blushed the color of squished up tomatoes.

This is what it said:

DEAR CLASS,

IF YOU'RE GOING TO VOTE FOR ME,

PLEASE VOTE FOR PETER CAVELLI

INSTEAD. THE COMPUTER CONTEST WAS

HIS IDEA. HE'D MAKE A GREAT PRESIDENT.

JUST MAKE ANOTHER BOX ON THE

BALLOT AND WRITE HIS NAME NEXT TO

IT. THEN CHECK OFF THE BOX. THANK YOU.

Samantha Smartypants

Book Discussion Questions

1) Have you ever had to make a speech in front of your class? How did it make you feel? What were you afraid would happen?

2) What would make you vote for a particular classmate for class president? Would you only vote for your friends?

3) What ideas can you come up with to raise money for a class project? Do you think a computer contest would be popular in your school?

4) Who is the current president of the United States? How often do we elect a new president?

5) Why do you think Lisa stopped being mad about losing the election?

6) Samantha likes to do everything herself. Do you think that is a good idea? Do you like to do things by yourself?

7) Why did Samantha wait so long to ask Peter to help her?

8) Samantha asked her classmates to write Peter's name on the ballot. Would you have done that? Why or why not?

9) Why did Lisa's and Bobby's campaign promises not work? What is important about making a promise to someone?

10) Some kids made fun of Samantha for being too smart. Do you ever see kids making fun of other kids? If somebody made fun of you, how would you feel?

11) Samantha liked books, Lisa liked fashion, and Bobby liked sports. Can you name other things that you and your classmates like to do? Do you think you can come up with one thing that everybody likes to do?

12) Would you have liked the snacks that Samantha and Peter ate? Are there healthy snacks that also taste good?

13) Do you think Peter was a good friend to Samantha? What makes someone a good friend?

14) Why do you think Samantha signed her name *Samantha Smartypants* instead of Samantha Pojanowski on her letter to the class?

Class Projects

1) Have a class election. Decide what the class president will be responsible for doing. Discuss what qualities the class thinks are important for a president. Set up ground rules to ensure that the election is fair.

2) Pick a charity that is important to your class or community. Ask the class to think up fundraising ideas. Set a fundraising goal. Plan the fundraiser with the class. Include students in advertising, set-up, running the event, and clean-up. Emphasize the importance of teamwork.

3) Talk about upcoming elections in the community, town, state, or federal government. Make a chart of the current elected officials and those that are running for office. Talk about how people learn about the candidates and why people vote for them.

4) Show TV commercials for two candidates running for office. Discuss what makes them effective or not. Have groups of students create and act out their own TV commercials.

5) Discuss the idea of a debate. Pick a topic that is important to the class. Have students select which side they want to represent or whether they want to be spectators. Form two teams. Each team will discuss how they will defend their position and then select a spokesperson. Allot a certain amount of time for each team to present. The students who are spectators can then vote based on which side was more persuasive.

About the Author

Barbara Puccia has written short stories, magazine articles, and web content in addition to the Samantha Smartypants chapter books. She has also worked as an elementary school teacher and computer programmer. Barbara loves reading and writing and gets to bring the joy of books into other people's lives at her job in a local library. Barbara lives with her husband in Ramsey, New Jersey and has two college-aged daughters who are the pride and joy of her life.

About the Cover Illustrator

Emma Kane recently graduated high school and is preparing to attend Alfred University as an Art major. This year, she won the Scholastic Gold Key award for one of her self-portraits. Emma enjoys using a variety of mediums and would someday like to become a special effects makeup artist. She draws much of her inspiration from anime and enjoys drawing anything from cats to zombies.

About the Content Illustrator

Natalie Puccia is a student at Virginia Commonwealth University Art School where she is majoring in Art Education, Painting and Printmaking and working on a minor in Art History. She is planning a career as an art teacher and works during the summer as an art counselor at a sleep away camp. Natalie has already sold one of her paintings, and is a published artist who designed her high school yearbook. She graciously agreed to help her mom out by illustrating Samantha Smartypants.